Have you read all the
Super Soccer Boy books?

Super Soccer Boy
and the Exploding Footballs

Super Soccer Boy
and the Evil Electronic Bunnies

Super Soccer Boy
and the Snot Monsters

Super Soccer Boy
and the Giant Slugs

Super Soccer Boy
and the Alien Invasion

Super Soccer Boy
and the Laser Ray Robbery

Super Soccer Boy
and the Raging Robots

Super Soccer Boy
and the Monster Mutants

Piccadilly Press

For Alan

First published in Great Britain in 2012 by
Piccadilly Press, a Templar/Bonnier publishing company
Deepdene Lodge, Deepdene Avenue,
Dorking, Surrey RH5 4AT

www.piccadillypress.co.uk

ISBN: 978 1 84812 247 5

3 5 7 9 10 8 6 4 2

Printed in the UK by CPI Group (UK),
Croydon, CR0 4YY
Cover design by Simon Davis
Cover illustration by Judy Brown

Chapter One

Dirty Defending

'Come on, Mini-Stars!'

Harry's little league team, the Middletown Mini-Stars, were playing an away game in the next town. Harry's dad, the Mini-Stars' coach, was shouting encouragement from the sideline.

'Watch out for that defender, Harry, he's a bit of a brute.'

A parent from the opposing team, the Sutton Scorchers, glared at Mr Gribble. Mr Gribble suspected, by the look of him, that he was the boy's dad.

The game was going OK, but the Scorchers obviously knew of Harry's reputation as a prolific (to put it mildly) scorer and were doing their best to mark him out of the game. Even so, Harry had still managed to score twice already and they were only ten minutes into the first half. Harry had been a freakishly amazing football player ever since he was struck by lightning during a weird electrical storm and was transformed into Super Soccer Boy. And now he used his super skills to prevent crimes and solve mysteries – as well as winning football matches of course!

Just then the 'brute' of a defender lunged in with a wild tackle and sent Harry flying.

'Ref! Did you see that? Come on, that has to be a yellow!' shouted a horrified Middletown parent.

Peep! went the referee's whistle. He gave a free kick on the halfway line and waved a yellow card in the air. The defender did not look pleased. His dad even less so.

Jake, Harry's best mate, stepped up to take the free kick. Harry zoomed at super soccer speed, Jake passed to him and Harry went to take a shot.

'Ooooof!' said Harry, as the same defender,

who'd positioned himself further up the pitch, barged straight into Harry, sending him flying once more.

Unfortunately, it was too late for Harry to pull out of the shot and it went sailing over the crossbar and, without a net to stop it, it just kept on going.

'Wow! Look at it go,' said the Scorchers' goalie.

OI! THAT COULD'VE TAKEN MY HEAD OFF!

By the time it reached the back of the playing field, it was slowing down, but not much. It dipped over a fence at the back of the field and disappeared from view.

Even more unfortunately for the Scorchers, it was the last straw for the referee, and the offending defender was sent off. The game continued with the spare match ball, but it was all downhill for the Scorchers. With one player down it was almost impossible for them to keep Harry out of the game. We won't mention the final score – all we need to know is that Harry's goal tally was into double figures, and then some.

At the end of the game, the Scorchers trudged off dejected as the Middletown Mini-Stars celebrated another victory.

Harry's dad was soon tidying stuff away and matching players to parents to make sure everyone got home safely.

'Dad,' said Harry, 'Jake and I are going to try and get the ball back.'

'OK,' Dad said, 'but don't climb over and break your neck or anything.'

'We'll do our best not to,' said Harry. He picked up his backpack, took out his pet rat, Ron (short for Ronaldo), and put him in the hood of his jacket. 'Come on, Jake, let's find that ball!'

Chapter Two

Weird Weeds

'That was some shot,' said Jake, 'or rather it would have been if that idiot hadn't barged you over. It went miles!'

'Sure did,' Harry said smiling. 'I hope we can find it though. Dad's pretty sick of the rate I get through footballs, although usually it's just that they fall apart because I kick them too hard.'

They reached the back of the playing field and looked up at the fence. It was very tall, with some nasty looking security wire along the top.

'I don't fancy my chances getting over that,' said Harry, 'and I didn't bring my Utility Boots.' Harry's Utility Boots were the special football boots he'd designed to help enhance his Super Soccer Boy skills.

He pushed apart some of the grass and weeds and peered through the fence.

'Those are some plants!' he exclaimed looking at the yard behind the fence. 'Let's see if we can find a gap.'

Harry and Jake felt their way along the fence in opposite directions. Harry was about to give up when Jake called out, 'Over here, Harry, give me a hand.'

Harry ran over and they both cleared away the undergrowth enough to give them access to a hole that was just big enough for them to crawl through.

'You can go first,' said Jake.

'Gee, thanks,' said Harry.

'Well, it was your shot – and your idea,' Jake said, laughing.

They squeezed through and found themselves standing in an empty factory yard that was

completely overgrown
with weeds.

Harry glanced up
at a large sign on the
side of the building.
'Fetherby's,' Harry
read. 'What is this
place?'

'It's part of the
old factory estate, I think,' said Jake. 'The place
my dad works used to have a warehouse here
somewhere, before they closed the whole estate
down. It was ages ago.'

Ron had jumped out of Harry's hoody and
was sniffing at the weeds.

'They're weird,' said Harry. 'I've never seen
any like that at Granddad's allotment.' Harry
often helped out his granddad on the allotment,
mainly because Granddad liked to talk about
football almost as much as Harry did and he
knew about all the old stars.

These plants had huge trumpet-like flowers which did remind him of a weed he'd seen before, but they were much, much bigger. They also had large round pods hanging down from them, which Harry assumed were full of seeds. The weeds were climbing the walls of the factory with long green tendrils, a bit like the ones you get on bean plants.

'Freaky-looking things!' said Harry. He took out his phone and snapped a picture to show his granddad.

'How on earth are we going to find the ball amongst all these weeds?' said Jake, kicking his way through the yard absent-mindedly.

Harry scanned the yard from left to right with his super soccer vision. 'There.' He pointed.

'Where?' said Jake. 'I can't see it.'

Harry trotted over to the far corner of the yard and fished the ball out from a pile of broken wooden pallets tangled up with weeds. He held it up triumphantly. 'Easy when you've got super soccer vision,' he said, smiling.

They turned to go back through the fence but Jake couldn't move his foot.

'Ow!' he said looking down.

One of the weed's tendrils was tangled around his ankle. He tried to pull it free but it was quite tight.

'How did you manage to do that?' asked
Harry.

'Dunno,' said Jake. 'Didn't even realise I had.'

Harry carefully untangled him.

'C'mon,' Harry said, scooping Ron up. 'Let's
get out of this place.'

Mr Gribble dropped Jake off at his house and
headed home to Crumbly Drive. Harry was
pleased when he saw that Granddad's car was
parked outside – he was dying to show him the
photo of the weird weed.

'Hi, Granddad!' he
said, bursting
through the
front door.

Granddad
gave him a
hug. 'How was
the match?' he
asked.

'It was OK,' said Harry, 'apart from nearly losing the ball.'

Harry told his granddad what had happened and showed him the pictures on his phone.

'Hmmm, strange. Never seen weeds like that before.' He peered closely at the photo. 'Looks a bit like bindweed but loads bigger – and bindweed doesn't have those pods. Where was it?'

'It was at the back of the playing field. Jake said it was an old factory estate or something. The big sign on the building said Fetherby's, I think.'

'Oh I know the place. It was an old plant fertiliser factory. Looks like it's a weed factory now!' Granddad chuckled. 'They're pulling it down to build a giant shopping centre soon.'

'Not another one,' groaned Mum. 'That's all they ever do these days. I remember when . . .'

Harry stopped listening. He knew exactly what Mum was going to start talking about and knew that he would be bored.

'Let's find some football to watch, Ron,' he said, and headed for the TV.

After they'd had tea, Granddad lost hopelessly to Harry on the Playstation and then he went home. Harry decided to do a quick bit of Googling before he went to bed.

He put *Fetherby's Fertiliser* into the search box and pressed *Enter*. Up popped a list of links. Harry clicked the top one.

'Aha!' he said as a page from the local newspaper opened.

MIDDLETOWN GUARDIAN

Factory forced to close

Another businesss hit by the recession
blah blah blah blah blah blah blah

Another link confirmed what Granddad had said.

MIDDLETOWN GUARDIAN

Work is about to begin on a brand new shopping centre not far from Middletown

There was also an old map of the factory estate, which showed what the factories around Fetherby's had been.

'Interesting,' said Harry. 'So there was a chemical factory next door. I wonder . . .' Harry thought back to what had happened a while

before with the giant slugs. 'Chemicals can be very dangerous.'

Ron stretched and yawned.

Harry caught the yawn. 'You're right, Ron. Time for bed.'

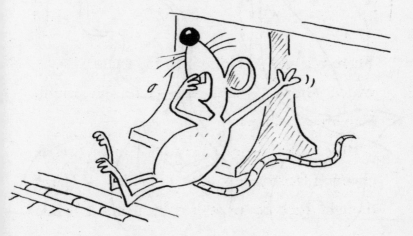

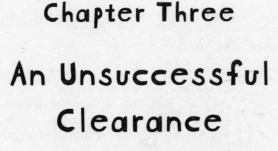

Chapter Three

An Unsuccessful Clearance

Harry had a very restless night. He dreamt that he and Jake were back at the factory looking for the ball, but in his dream the weeds were much more scary and threatening. They attacked Jake, binding him up. Then they went for Harry, grabbing his hands and feet. That was when he woke up shouting and found himself totally tangled in his duvet and sweating like he was in a sauna.

Ron looked really worried, and his whiskers twitched like mad.

'Ergh, what a horrible dream,' said Harry groggily. He looked at Ron's worried face. 'It's OK, Ron, just a bad dream. That's what happens if you go to bed when your imagination is working overtime.'

Meanwhile, at the factory, two huge lorries drove through the old, rusty main gates and stopped in the yard. They were followed by a large white van, out of which piled a dozen

burly workmen. They began to unload
equipment from the back of the lorries.

Someone in a different coloured hard hat was
ordering everyone about. 'OK, Bill. First things
first. We need to clear this yard for the skips to
come in.'

'Right, Fred.'

'Wayne – you, Eddie and Winston get going with the strimmers while I sort out the weed killer.'

'OK,' said Wayne, yawning. He wandered over to the back of one of the lorries and pulled out an industrial-sized strimmer, the kind that councils use. 'Oi! Winston, Eddie, over 'ere.'

Two of the workmen strolled towards Wayne, who was pulling two more strimmers out of the lorry. They carried the machines over to the densest part of the weedy undergrowth.

'Goggles on. Ready, lads? OK, fire 'em up!'

Wayne, Winston and Eddie lined up and started their strimmers.

27

There was total panic.

'Somebody call 999!' yelled Bill.

Chapter Four

Dreams Can Come True

When the news came on the TV, Harry and Ron were eating breakfast.

'A report just coming in,' said the newsreader. 'There has been an incident at a disused factory estate in Middletown. Workmen clearing the site have been taken to hospital. Over to our reporter, Nadeen Ahmed, who is at the factory gate.'

'Thank you, Kate!' said a very excited-sounding but stern-faced reporter. 'I am standing only metres from where the incident took place.'

Harry looked up, amazed to see the very factory that he and Jake had been standing outside the previous afternoon.

'Mum! MUM!' called Harry. 'Listen to this!'

'From what I have heard,' continued the reporter, 'fantastic though it may sound, the workmen said they had been attacked by the very plants they were trying to clear.'

Harry spat a mouthful of choccy hoops across the table. Ron ducked just in time.

'It . . . I . . . my dream!' he garbled.

'Oh Harry, that's disgusting. Clear it up,' said Mum.

'Gusting!' Harry's sister, Daisy, chimed in, laughing at the soggy mess.

'Sorry, but that's where we were yesterday,

Mum. Those are the plants I showed Granddad.'

The excited reporter continued, looking like she was about to burst. 'Three workmen have been taken to hospital with what has been described as an allergic reaction to the plants. The rest of the workforce have simply downed tools and left the site. That's all I can tell you for now, Kate. The hospital is due to issue a statement later this afternoon.'

Brrrring.

Mum's mobile rang. Harry started switching between channels, desperate for more information.

'I thought those plants were freaky, Mum,' Harry said.

His mum didn't answer.

'MUM!' he said louder, but she was on the phone, deep in conversation.

'Shush, Harry, wait a moment,' she said

holding her hand up to stop him from interrupting again. 'Yes, of course, Cynthia, no problem. Anything I can do to help. No problem at all. Yes . . . yes . . . and I'll give her tea before I bring her back . . . Of course . . . Give him my love . . . Bye.'

She hung up. 'Well, I never! What a shock!'

'MUM! WHAT?!' said Harry impatiently.

'Oh yes, Harry, that was Cynthia. Daisy's friends with her daughter at nursery. Her hubbie Wayne is one of the workmen at the factory. She was just asking me to pick Daisy's friend up from nursery and bring her back with Daisy. Cynthia's stuck at the hospital with Wayne, poor thing.'

'Is he OK?' asked Harry.

'Well, yes, er, mostly, it seems. She couldn't say much,' said Mum, clearly keeping something to herself. 'Anyway, you'd better get off to school, you'll be late.'

'Yes, Mum,' said Harry.

Harry met Jake on the corner as usual and they walked to school. Jake had heard the news as well.

'So, Jake, shall we go back to the factory and check it out after school?'

'Er, no, thank you very much. Look at this.' Jake pulled up his trouser leg to show Harry his ankle. There was a thick green stripe around it.

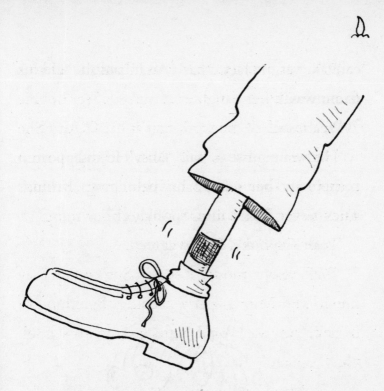

'Wow!' said Harry.

'Yes, I'm beginning to wonder whether it was me getting tangled or the plant tangling me. I'm thinking that it was a lucky escape after what's happened this morning.'

Harry couldn't argue with that.

'Anyway my mum says it's haunted.'

'Haunted?!' Harry laughed.

'No joke, Harry. Apparently there was an old

caretaker at the factory. Mr Archibald she said his name was.'

'Yeah, so?'

'He went missing,' said Jake. 'He disappeared completely but left all his belongings behind. They never found him. Spooky, eh?'

'Yeah – spooky,' Harry agreed.

Chapter Five

Jolly Green Giant

School seemed to drag on even longer than usual, probably because Harry was dying to get home. He couldn't even concentrate at football practice and Mr Blunt had a go at him for messing about.

'Come on, Harry, get your head together or

you can stay after practice and clear up.'

'Sorry, sir,' said Harry – that was the last thing he wanted.

When he and Jake eventually did leave, Harry was in such a hurry that Jake could hardly keep up.

HANG ON, HARRY!

'Where's the fire?' asked Jake.

'Just in a hurry to get back. Daisy's friend will be there.'

'Er, what? You weird or something? Since when were you interested in hanging out with your sister and her three-year-old friends?'

'She might know something about her dad and the plants.'

'Yeah,' said Jake, 'and a lot of sense a three year old is going to make. Good luck with that.'

Jake had a point.

'Better than nothing! See you tomorrow,' said Harry, and darted off.

Harry opened his front door. 'I'm home!' he called.

Two excited three year olds came bounding into the hall screaming and giggling. Daisy's friend Esmee went to Harry and jumped up and down on the spot.

'My daddy's gone green!' she said excitedly. 'Green all over, even his hair. Hee hee hee. He's a jolly green giant.'

Daisy and Esmee exploded with laughter and ran out into the back garden, where they stomped around hysterically doing jolly-green-giant impressions.

'O . . . K . . .' said Harry, and went inside to check any news updates.

'Hi, Mum,' he said.

His mum was already watching the TV – the local news was on.

'A hospital statement . . .' said the still-excited reporter from the morning news – she was revelling in her day in the spotlight. 'We are told that the workmen are shortly going to be released from hospital. Doctors say that apart from a strange pigmentation, all tests seem to show that they are fit and well. It is hoped that the pigmentation will fade over the next twenty-four to forty-eight hours.

'Such a relief,' said Harry's mum. 'Cynthia just rang to say they'll be home in an hour or two, so I'll give Esmee some tea with Daisy, then I'll walk her home.'

'I can do that if you like,' said Harry.

'Oh that would be really helpful, Harry. I've got nothing done today with those two tearing around. Aren't you a sweetheart?' She hugged him enthusiastically and Harry felt a bit guilty. He'd only offered so that he could try and get a look at Esmee's dad. Still, it didn't do any harm for Mum to think he was just being thoughtful.

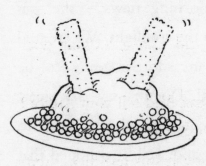

After fish fingers, mashed potato and peas – Esmee's favourite apparently – it was time for her to go home. Harry set off with one three year old holding tightly to each hand. They were beside themselves with the excitement of Harry walking them to Esmee's house.

'Now, be super good for Harry and do just what he says,' said Mum.

'Yes, Mrs Dribble,' said Esmee, looking doe-eyed at Harry.

'Er, that's *Gribble*, dear. And tell your daddy I hope he feels better soon.'

Fortunately for Harry, it was less than a ten-minute walk to Esmee's house. When they arrived, Harry was pleased to see that Wayne, her dad, was standing in the front garden waiting. He was indeed green, from head to toe.

'Harry! Your mum rang to say you were on your way. Good of you to drop Esmee home,' he said.

'No trouble,' said Harry. 'Hope you're feeling OK.'

Esmee ran and hugged her dad.

'I'm fine, Harry, never better. Lovely evening, isn't it?'

'Er, yes, I suppose it is.' *Well, it's not raining at least*, thought Harry, *but hardly what he'd have called a nice evening.*

Esmee's mum joined them outside.

'Come on, Esmee, bathtime. Are you coming in, Wayne?' she asked. 'You've been out here ages and it's getting chilly. You should really come in and get some rest.'

'I'm fine out here, enjoying the fresh air,' said Wayne. 'I'll come in soon, maybe.' He looked up at the cloudy sky and smiled contentedly.

'Bye, then,' said Harry.

'Bye, Ezzie,' said Daisy.

They turned to go.

'He's so greeeen,' chuckled Daisy. 'It's funny!'

'Funny . . . yes,' said Harry.

But Harry was wondering why Wayne was so keen to stand outside in the chilly garden. Maybe he was just enjoying the fact he was feeling OK after the scare this morning. Harry's super soccer senses, though, were telling him something different.

Chapter Six

The Root
of the Problem

Next morning, Harry was awoken by his
mother's voice. She was talking breathlessly on
the phone.

'Yes, Cynthia, I'll be round as soon as I've
dressed ... Yes, yes ... I know ... Try not to worry,
Cyn ... I'm sure everything will be fine ... I'll be

there in ten.' She hung up. 'Oh dear, oh dear!' She sounded really flustered.

Harry opened his door. His mum was dashing around like a maniac.

'What's going on?'

'Can't talk now, put the news on, it's Wayne, got to go, bye!' And she was out of the door with almost super soccer speed.

'That doesn't sound good, Ron.' Harry grabbed Ron, went downstairs and turned on the TV. Daisy was on the sofa eating her way through a packet of biscuits, which Mum had seemingly been in too much of a panic to notice before she left.

'. . . and I've been here since five this morning.' Nadeen, the reporter, was evidently working overtime. 'From what I can see, Wayne Withers has literally taken root in the front garden.

Daisy dropped her biscuit. 'He's greener,' she said. 'He's got leaves.'

She was right, he did have leaves. He also had
tendrils that covered the garden and were
spreading over the wall and up the front of the
house. Then the camera was pushed away as
police began to clear the area of reporters and
put an evidence tent up to shield Wayne Withers

from prying eyes. Harry could see, though, that plants like the ones at the factory had started to pop up all over the lawn.

The reporter was interviewing Mrs Withers, Esmee's mum, who was understandably distraught.

'I told Wayne to come inside, but he wouldn't listen. I didn't know what to do.' She sniffed. 'He just kept saying, "Ten more minutes, then I'll come in." I fell asleep. Then when I woke up, I came out here and well . . . he's . . .' She burst into tears.

Suddenly someone Harry recognised burst into shot.

'You people, leave this poor woman alone. Hasn't she got enough to deal with without you shoving cameras in her face?' With that, Harry's mum bundled her friend into the house.

'Yay, Mum! Way to go!' cheered Harry.

He wondered what had happened to the other two workmen.

'People are wondering about the other two

workmen. Paul, you have news about that.'

'Yes, Nadeen,' said another reporter in another location very familiar to Harry. 'I'm standing at the edge of Middletown Common. A police tent has been erected in the centre of the common and it is believed that inside the tent stands

Winston Gardner, second of the three workmen admitted to hospital yesterday after an allergic reaction. Mr Gardner has actually taken root on the common and a strange plant, unknown to experts, seems to be spreading around him.'

The reporter turned
to a red-faced
policeman who was
standing a few steps
away.

'I have here Inspector
Button who is in charge
of the operation.
Inspector, what can you tell us about these plants?

'Er, well, at the moment, the situation is unclear.'

'Have you tried removing the plants?'

'Yes we have. It appears, however, that doing so seems to cause the gentleman, er, considerable discomfort.'

Harry, with his super soccer hearing, could hear the 'considerable discomfort' in the background.

'Ouch! No, ooh, don't you dare! You — ouch stop that! Ow. OW!'

He could also see that the more Mr Gardner

was shouting, the more the tendrils flailed around, as if to protect him.

'Doctors are with Mr Gardner at the moment, er, assessing the situation,' said the inspector.

'But you can't see Mr Gardner being moved at the moment.'

'Er, no. We think it best at this time to, erm, keep Mr Gardner contained on the common and as comfortable as possible.'

In other words, thought Harry, *you can't!*

'Thank you, Inspector. The other workman from yesterday's strange incident remains missing. Back to the studio.'

Daisy looked up at her brother. 'What's happening, Harry?'

55

'Daisy,' he said, 'that's a very good question.'

One thing was clear. This was a job for:

Chapter Seven

Pop, Pop, Pop

'Jake, we need to go back to the factory before this gets any more out of hand.' Harry had rung Jake as soon as he'd finished watching the news report.

'I was afraid that was why you were ringing me so early,' said Jake. 'But it's dangerous, Harry.'

'I think the weeds only attack if you attack them first. Perhaps you trampled on the tendrils and they just wound around you to stop you doing it.'

'Hmmm.' Jake thought back to how he'd kicked the plants out of his way. 'Maybe . . . I suppose. They didn't actually do anything to me.'

'So if we're careful not to harm them, we should be safe,' said Harry brightly. 'And I'm going to ask Granddad if he'll come too, being the plant expert.'

'Oh, all right then.' Jake always found it hard to say no to Harry. 'I guess it will be OK.'

'Great! I'll ring Granddad now.'

Granddad was more than happy to come

along and five minutes later he arrived at Harry's house. Next stop was Jake's house before the short journey to the playing field where Harry and Jake had played football only two days before.

Police were stopping people driving down the road to the factory estate but fortunately Harry and Jake knew another way in. It took a bit of grunting and groaning to make the hole in the fence big enough to get Granddad through, but soon the three of them were standing in the factory yard.

'Wow!' said Jake.

The two lorries that had arrived there the days before were now completely swallowed up by the weeds.

'I can't believe how fast they've grown.'

'Faster than the fastest growing bamboo, and that grows a metre a day,' said Granddad. 'This

must be more like a metre an hour!'

'If you watch it,' said Harry, 'you can actually *see* it growing.'

'It's AMAZING!' said Granddad. 'I want to get a closer look at one of those pods.'

'Careful, Granddad, you mustn't tread on any of the plants, the leaves or the tendrils.'

They did their best to walk through the yard, but there was almost nowhere they could put their feet without treading on something.

'This isn't going to work,' said Harry. 'You two stay here. It's a good job I wore my Utility Boots. I'll use them to get a better look.'

Jake breathed a sigh of relief. 'Right you are, Harry,' he said. 'Did you hear that?' he asked Granddad.

'Yes, yes . . .' Granddad's voice drifted off as he stared in fascination at the plant pods.

Harry set his boots to *Hover* mode and moved

over to the pods which clung to the factory walls. He glanced in the window.

'Oh ... my ... God,' said Harry quietly. 'You guys, you have to see this. Oh wait, you can't. Hang on.' Harry took his phone out of his pocket and took a few pictures, flash off, just in case it disturbed the plant.

Inside the factory, Harry could see a giant version of the weed from which all the others had seemed to spread. 'Awesome,' he said.

Suddenly he heard Jake shouting. 'No, Granddad! NO! DON'T!'

Harry turned around to see what was happening.

'GRANDDAD! NO!' Harry echoed, seeing what his granddad was about to do. 'The plant, it will —'

But it was too late.

Granddad's curiosity had got the better of him — he was trying to take a cutting.

'I'm sure one little shoot won't hurt. Just one . . .' There was a *pop, pop, popping* sound and a pod exploded all over Granddad, showering him

in little spikes. Jake tried to go and help but
tendrils quickly had him pinned down.

'Hold on, Granddad!' said Harry. He zoomed
over at super soccer speed just as another pod
started to make the popping sound.

BOOF! Harry
booted it before it
had a chance to
explode and the
shoot withered
away. *Boof! BOOF!*
He booted another
two pods, which

were about to burst, scooped Jake and Granddad up and scrambled over the fence.

The three of them lay in a heap in the playing field.

'Granddad, are you OK?' asked Harry.

'I'm fine, Harry. Absolutely fine!' But Jake and Harry could see he was already turning green.

'We'd better get back to my house,' said Harry. 'Are you all right to drive?'

'Course I am, Harry,' said Granddad.

They drove back to Harry's in silence. It had just started to rain.

'Sunshine and showers,' said Granddad happily. 'The perfect weather for weeds.'

Harry and Jake looked at each other, nervously.

Chapter Eight

Granddad Green

'Oh my days!' shrieked Harry's mum when they
got back.

'Don't worry, dear, I feel fine,' said Granddad.

'But you're all GREEN! Harry!' She turned
to him furiously. 'You shouldn't have gone back,
and you shouldn't have got Granddad involved

too. Sometimes I just . . . despair!'

'It'll be OK, Mum,' said Harry, feeling really guilty. 'Granddad will be fine as long as we keep him indoors, away from the soil.'

'I'm sure Harry's right,' said Jake. Actually he wasn't sure at all but felt he needed to back up his friend.

'All I need now,' said Granddad, 'is a nice cup of tea.' He smiled reassuringly.

Harry started picking off some of the little spikes that were still stuck in Granddad's skin.

'What are you doing, Harry?' asked Jake.

'I need to see how sharp these are. How much protection we'll need when we go back.'

'When we *what*?!' queried Jake.

Harry set the spikes down for a moment and showed Jake the pictures he took of the inside of the factory. 'Look!'

'That's incredible,' gasped Jake. 'The size of that thing! It looks like all of the plants are —'

'Coming from that one? I thought so too. I have to go back. What happened to those workmen will probably happen to my granddad. I have to find a way to stop it, and I think that's where I'll find it.' He looked glum. 'It's my fault Granddad got zapped.'

'Not entirely, Harry, he did try and break off a piece of the plant.'

'Yes, I know, but Mum's right – I should never have got him involved.'

Jake looked at Harry with an expression of sudden realisation. 'Hey, Harry, you know that caretaker who went missing?'

Harry looked at Jake and nodded.

'Do you think he might have something to do with it?'

'Yes,' said Harry. 'I do.'

...SOMETHING WAS HAPPENING TO THE PLANT

THE MUTANT FLOWER SUDDENLY GREW, IT SWALLOWED UP POOR ARCHIE ARCHIBALD.

72

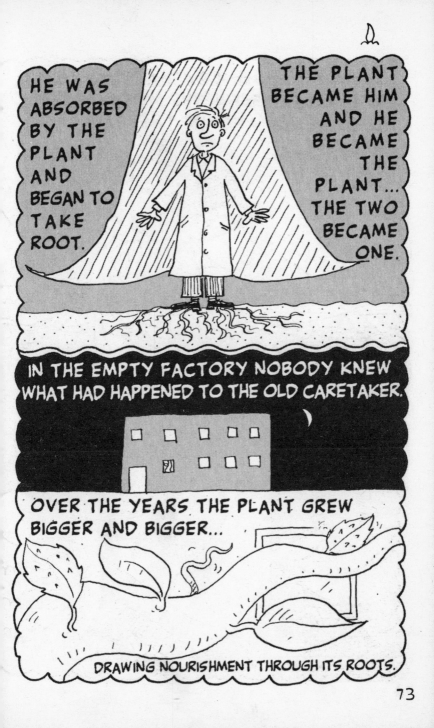

73

Chapter Nine

From Bad
To Worse . . .

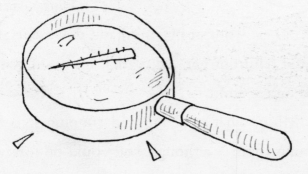

Harry had spent the rest of the evening studying the plant spikes. It was very late when he eventually got to sleep. He didn't get long to recharge his batteries either.

'Aaaaaargh!' came an anguished yell from downstairs. It was his mum.

Harry looked at his clock – six a.m. 'That sounds bad, Ron,' said Harry. 'Aaaaaaaargh!' screamed Mum again. 'Granddad!' Harry dashed out of his room and downstairs. He could tell from her yelling that his mum was in the dining room.

'Mum, what is it?' he said running into the dining room – although you could be forgiven now if you'd mistaken it for the garden.

Granddad was standing in the corner of the room. He'd pulled out a plant from a large pot, climbed into it and taken root. Harry's mum was frantic.

'Look at your granddad, Harry. What are we going to do?'

'I'll fix this,' said Harry. 'I promise. I'd better ring Jake, see if he's still OK.' He doubted whether Jake would be awake yet but he just couldn't wait.

'What . . . Harry it's six o'clock in the morning, what's going on?' said a sleepy Jake.

'Are you OK?'

'Er, yes, I think so. Apart from the green stripe around my ankle, a few other green splodges and the fact that I've just been woken at an unearthly hour, but otherwise . . . Why?'

'It's my granddad.' Harry explained what had happened.

'Oh no! I bet your mum is mad.'

'Just a bit,' said Harry. 'I'm going for a ride around the town to see what's happening to the others. Then I'm coming over to you, OK?'

'OK, Harry.' Jake could hear in Harry's voice that he was upset about his granddad. 'You'll sort it out, Harry, you always do. Just give me a chance to get washed and have breakfast – I'm starving.'

'Cool,' said Harry. 'See you soon.'

Ten minutes later, Harry had washed and dressed and was out of the door. He wasn't really hungry enough for breakfast, but he gave Ron some cornflakes and put him in his hoody for company.

'We're going for a ride, Ron.'

First Harry cycled over to Esmee's house. He couldn't believe what he saw. He parked his bike over the road and looked up.

'Good job I wore my Utility Boots, Ron,' he said, switching them to *Hover*.

Harry rose up above the house and gasped at the sight below. The monster mutant weeds had entirely covered the house and pods were

forming all over it. It looked like one had
popped in the garden and zapped a cat. The
bewildered creature was standing in the middle
of the lawn. It had taken root, just like

Granddad
and the
workmen
and
tendrils
radiated
from it
in all
directions.
Harry
snapped some photos
to show Jake, and then said to Ron, 'Let's go and
see what's happening on the common.'

He pedalled over to the common and stared
in amazement. The common was totally
surrounded by a circle of police. The overnight
rain had enabled the weeds to spread even faster
than they had at the factory. As Harry watched,
tendrils started to wind themselves around some
of the policemen on guard.

'Oi,' Harry heard one of them say. 'Get off

POP

POP

83

me.' The officer automatically pulled at the plant and broke off the tendril. Immediately, there was a loud *pop*, *pop*, *pop* and several of the policemen were caught in a shower of spikes.

'Ron, we're in trouble,' Harry said, snapping more pictures. 'These plants could take over the world. I have to do something – and quickly.'

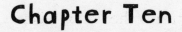

Chapter Ten

. . . and Worse

Harry pedalled at super soccer speed to Jake's house.

'Hi, Harry,' said Jake. 'You feeling OK? You look awful.'

'So would you if you'd been where I have this morning. Those weeds are spreading like . . .

well, weeds. Monster mutant weeds, in fact. We need to make a plan.'

'Did you hear about the missing workman?' asked Jake.

'No,' said Harry.

'They found him at last. He'd gone to some friends for dinner in the evening after he was released from hospital. It looks like he got halfway home, then parked the car in a supermarket car park and took root around the back,' said Jake. 'When they went to open up this morning, the manager couldn't even get to the door.'

'This is bad,' said Harry, shaking his head. His stomach rumbled.

'Come in and have some breakfast,' said Jake.

'I'm not really hungry,' said Harry.

'Well, your stomach is, I can hear it. Anyway, you'll need the energy.'

RRUMBLE!!!

'Oh, OK.'

Harry trudged into the kitchen and sat at the kitchen table while Jake made some toast.

'Look at the pictures I took this morning,' said Harry.

'Whoa!' said Jake. 'Those things have really gone wild.'

'I expect all of those policemen will have been zapped by now. And the more people that get zapped by the popping pods, the faster the plant will spread.'

Jake suddenly felt a bit sick.

But just then Harry's face brightened. Something had suddenly occurred to him. Maybe it was the toast feeding his brain.

'Hey, Jake. You remember at the factory, when I kicked those pods?'

'Yes, when they were about to pop, you mean?'

'Yeah, that part of the plant died, didn't it? Sort of withered away.'

'Yes, you're right it did, I remember now,' agreed Jake. 'We were in such a panic to get away that I'd completely forgotten.'

'Me too. And if we could get inside the factory, to that biggest mutant plant, and burst the pods on that the same way . . .'

'It might wither and die too!' said Jake. 'I like your thinking! The only trouble is, though, how on earth do we get in without being zapped. There are so many pods, you couldn't possibly burst them all, even if you are Super Soccer Boy.'

'Aha! That's where my spike research comes in.' Harry took a sheet of paper out of his pocket and spread it on the table. 'Look. I tried different materials to find something that would protect us from the spikes.'

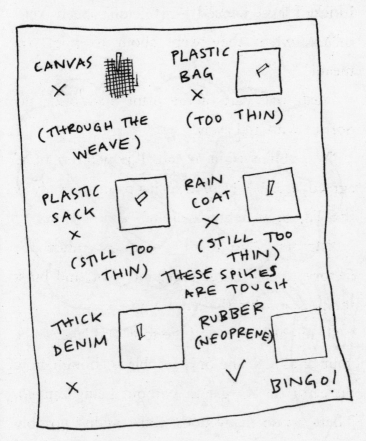

CANVAS
X
(THROUGH THE WEAVE)

PLASTIC BAG
X
(TOO THIN)

PLASTIC SACK
X
(STILL TOO THIN)

RAIN COAT
X
(STILL TOO THIN)
THESE SPIKES ARE TOUGH

THICK DENIM
X

RUBBER (NEOPRENE)
√
BINGO!

Jake examined the results of Harry's experiments. 'Rubber?' he said.

'Like a wetsuit, for instance!' Harry smiled. 'You've got one, haven't you?'

'Yes, from holiday last year when we all tried surfing.' Jake winced – it hadn't been very successful.

'And I've got one too. Before I became Super Soccer Boy, I couldn't stay in the sea for more than two minutes without freezing to death. The only thing I haven't got is a mask, though.'

'That's no problem.' Jake ran into the hall and started chucking stuff out of the cupboard under the stairs, which, like the one in Harry's house, was full of junk. He came back in the kitchen triumphantly. 'Here!' He was holding two snorkelling masks.

'Brilliant!' said Harry. 'Let's go back to my house and get ready.' He picked Ron up from the table. 'And we need to go past the corner shop – we'll need some rubber gloves to protect our hands. Hmm. What can I do about you, Ron?' pondered Harry.

MEANWHILE...

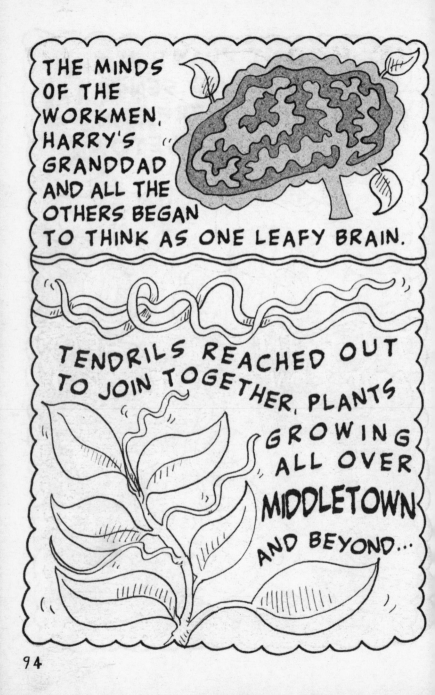

THE MINDS OF THE WORKMEN, HARRY'S GRANDDAD AND ALL THE OTHERS BEGAN TO THINK AS ONE LEAFY BRAIN.

TENDRILS REACHED OUT TO JOIN TOGETHER, PLANTS GROWING ALL OVER **MIDDLETOWN** AND BEYOND...

95

Chapter Eleven

Battle Plans

Back at Harry's house, they prepared for battle. Jake had brought his Nerf Blaster with him and was doing some target practice, while Harry sorted out their protective gear.

'Bullseye!' said Jake as he scored a direct hit on one of Daisy's toy bunnies.

'Don't let Daisy see you do that – she'll never forgive you,' said Harry.

'I've got to practise on something for popping those pods. I won't be able to kick them like you,' said Jake.

'What do you think?' said Harry, holding up a rubber glove with peculiar holes cut out of it.

'What on earth is that?' asked Jake.

'It's for Ron,' said Harry. 'He usually comes in handy in these situations and if he's coming he'll need protection too. You saw the photo of what happened to the cat in Esmee's garden.'

'Good point.'

Harry put the rubber suit on Ron the rat.

'It doesn't cover all of you but it should be enough – you're a pretty small target,' he said. 'So that's it, everything ready. Let's get suited up.'

Harry poked his head around the door of the

dining room. Granddad's weeds were almost into the hall.

'Don't worry, Granddad. We're going to sort out this mutant mess.' Granddad smiled. 'Come on, Jake. It's time to go.'

★ ★ ★

Twenty minutes later, Harry and Jake, dressed head to toe in rubber, were speeding through the streets of Middletown. They were quite a peculiar sight. Harry had Ron and his football in his backpack and Jake was armed with his Nerf Blaster ammo belt.

Jake was nervous. Even Harry had a few butterflies – he was worried about his granddad. Their nerves weren't helped by what they saw as they pedalled to the factory.

'Harry!' shouted Jake. 'Look at that!'

'I'm looking, I'm looking.'

All along the high street near the common, people had taken root in whatever patch of earth they could find. They were on the grass verges, in the flowerbeds, someone was even sitting in a window box. Flowers and pods were already

beginning to form all over the plants. It was an eerie sight. It was only then that it occurred to Harry that the streets and roads, apart from the people who were growing, were almost deserted. *It won't be long before the road is blocked by the weeds,* thought Harry.

It was worse out of town, where zapped people had taken root and the weeds had fields to spread through. The whole area was covered with a thick blanket of green and, as they rode along, they could hear the *pop, pop, pop* of bursting pods. Jake began to wonder if it was already too late.

They arrived at the playing field and parked their bikes near the pavilion. The playing field itself was still clear.

'Are you ready for this?' Harry asked.

'Ready as I'll ever be,' said Jake.

'OK, then, piggyback time.' Harry turned his Utility Boots to *Hover* mode once more and, with Jake on his back, he rose over the fence and landed as gently as he could in the yard. Plants, tendrils and pods moved around them, sensing their presence. It was as if they instinctively knew that Harry and Jake were up to no good. The factory was now completely covered – it looked like a huge square tangle of weeds.

'There's no way in,' said Jake.

Harry concentrated and, with his super soccer vision, he could just make out a door next to the window he'd been looking in the day before.

'There's a door over there,' Harry pointed. 'We need to make a path to it.'

'Gulp!' gulped Jake.

They moved forward, Harry leading the way.

Pop, pop, POP! went the pods.

Then Harry made his move.

Boof! Boof! BOOF! He darted about with super soccer speed, twisting and turning, scissor-kicking here, back-flipping there, kicking pods into kingdom come. But then he realised that not all of the plants were withering. Jake was randomly shooting his Nerf gun, but none of the plants shoots were dying!

Harry watched closely, and then realised that timing was everything.

'Wait for the third pop!' yelled Harry. 'Then shoot!'

'Got it!' said Jake withering his first bit of plant.

But even with his super soccer strength, Harry was getting worn out. There were just so  many pods to pop and they couldn't get them all before they popped. Showers of spikes bounced off their wetsuits and onto the ground. It seemed hopeless.

Gradually Harry managed to clear a narrow path to the factory door. Jake followed behind. Tendrils waved everywhere, trying to grab them, and as they got closer to the door, the tendrils from the walls and roof of the building directed themselves at the invaders.

'Help!' yelled Jake.

Harry turned. Jake had been grabbed by four different tendrils, one ensnaring each limb. It was all he could do to hang onto his blaster. Harry really didn't want to think about what might happen if they all began to pull in different directions.

Harry dashed over to try and get him free but as he did, the path he'd made began to close behind him.

'No, Harry!' said Jake. 'You have to go on. I'll be OK. Get that mutant monster!'

Harry was torn. He knew the sensible thing was to do as Jake had told him, but he didn't want to abandon him.

'I'll leave Ron here with you – he might be able to do something.'

Harry took Ron out of the backpack and set him down. Ron scampered over to Jake and, seeing that he was trapped, instantly began to gnaw at the tendrils.

Harry turned and ran for the factory door at super soccer speed. He shoulder-barged it open and stood inside the factory.

'Awesome!' Harry said.

Chapter Twelve

Harry vs Monster Mutant

Harry had never seen anything like it. The main stem was more like a trunk – it was almost three metres thick. Harry was frozen to the spot by the sheer size of the mutant monster and its swaying tendrils. But he didn't stay frozen for long.

'Argh!' A huge, thick, hairy tendril flailed at

him. He dodged out of the way as if dodging a tackle. 'Can't catch me!' he taunted.

But that was just the beginning. Harry detected movement above him, and looked up.

'Oh dear,' he said. 'That looks like trouble.'

The tendrils that covered the walls and ceiling moved towards him. It took all his super tackle-dodging skills to avoid them. He tried to pop some of the pods too but it was almost impossible to dodge and burst pods at the same time. Then it came to him what he should do.

'OK, you want me? Then catch me!' Harry

started to run around the trunk of the monster mutant. Not too fast at first, just so the tendrils would follow. Gradually he sped up. Faster and faster he went around the trunk. Faster and faster the tendrils followed him – until they were totally tangled around the massive trunk. It was wrapped up like a mummy! All the pods were now squeezed together – it looked like some bizarre Christmas tree.

'I've got you now!' said Harry.

Pods were *pop, pop, popping* all over the place. Harry dashed like a demon striker booting the popping pods. Plant shoots began to wither and drop off as Harry made his way around the base of the trunk. Then he took out his football.

'I can't reach the higher ones,' Harry said. 'It's football time!'

BOOF! BOOF! BOOF! went the football as bits of leaf and tendril littered the floor. It was great target practice.

'Hey, Harry!' said a familiar voice behind him. 'Can I join in?'

'Jake!' he cheered. 'Be my guest.'

Ron darted in behind him, still gnawing on the last of the tendrils that had captured Jake.

Obviously they were quite tasty, although to be honest, Ron would eat just about anything.

Jake loaded his Nerf Blaster, and between the two of them, they popped the rest of the pods. It was even more satisfying than popping bubble wrap.

By the time they were down to the last few pods, Jake was out of ammo and it was up to Harry to finish the job. *BOOF! BOOF! BOOF! CRACK!!!!!*

There was a massive cracking, crunching sound, and the monster mutant trunk started to split in two from the top.

'It's going, Harry!' said Jake, stepping backwards out of the way.

The crack spread gradually down the trunk and bits fell off and crumbled away as it went. *CRASH!!!*

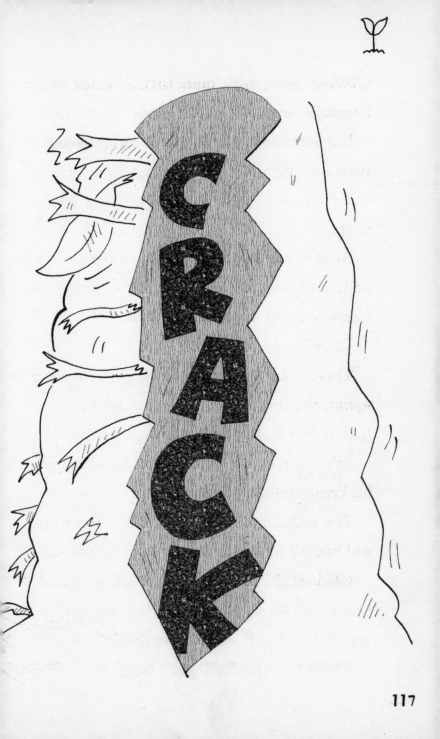

With one final crunch, the trunk split completely in two and collapsed.

'I don't believe it,' said Jake when he looked at what was left.

Inside the remains stood an extremely bewildered looking old man. His clothes were rags and his beard was long and grey.

'Hello, Mr Archibald,' said Harry.

'So that's what happened to the old caretaker,' said Jake.

'Yep. I was hoping we'd find him in there. Poor soul, he's going to get a bit of a shock when he finds out how long he was imprisoned.'

'And how big he'd grown!' laughed Jake. 'Do you think all the other plants will have died too?'

'I certainly hope so,' said Harry.

They went outside. The plant around the factory had definitely gone the same way as the one inside. It was brittle underfoot and just snapped as they walked across the factory yard, helping Mr Archibald take his first steps for five years.

'We'd better call an ambulance, for matey here,' said Jake, looking at the dazed old man blinking in the daylight.

'I guess we had,' said Harry. He got out his mobile and pressed 999.

Final score
Harry 1,000,000
– Monster Mutant 0

All over Middletown, the monster mutants withered, died and crumbled. Dazed people pulled up their brittle roots and shook their heads in disbelief. At Crumbly Drive, Granddad Gribble stepped out of the plant pot and stretched.

'Well done, Harry,' he said. 'You've saved us all!'

HARRY'S F⚽⚽TBALL FACTS!

When Malta played England in 1971, it was so one-sided,

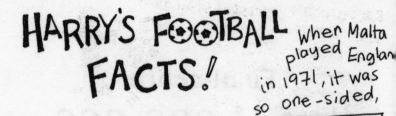

Brazil have won the world cup 5 times, but they've never won the Olympic gold! (Not yet anyway)

Gordon Banks didn't have one shot to save.

In 1997 Bury players refused to do any more promotional work as a protest at the lack of nappy changing facilities for their wives.

Neil Armstrong originally wanted to take a football to the moon.

Barcelona's Hristo Stoichkov was banned for 6 months in 1990 for stamping on the referee's foot after being sent off.

Referee Henning Erikstrup was about to blow full time in a Danish league match when his false teeth fell out!

In 1997 Nigerian international Babayaro, broke his leg while celebrating a goal in his Chelsea debut game.

And it was only a pre-season friendly!

Luigi Riva once broke a spectator's arm with one of his powerful shots. OUCH!

Join
Super Soccer Boy
online:

www.supersoccerboy.com

⚽ Fun activities
⚽ Football facts and quiz
⚽ All the latest
on the books
⚽ And much more!